# The Magic Factory
## MIDSUMMER MAGIC

# The Magic Factory
## MIDSUMMER MAGIC

## THERESA BRESLIN

**OXFORD**
UNIVERSITY PRESS

# OXFORD
UNIVERSITY PRESS

Great Clarendon Street, Oxford OX2 6DP

Oxford University Press is a department of the University of Oxford.
It furthers the University's objective of excellence in research, scholarship,
and education by publishing worldwide in

Oxford New York

Auckland Cape Town Dar es Salaam Hong Kong Karachi
Kuala Lumpur Madrid Melbourne Mexico City Nairobi
New Delhi Shanghai Taipei Toronto

With offices in

Argentina Austria Brazil Chile Czech Republic France Greece
Guatemala Hungary Italy Japan Poland Portugal Singapore
South Korea Switzerland Thailand Turkey Ukraine Vietnam

Oxford is a registered trade mark of Oxford University Press
in the UK and in certain other countries

British Library Cataloguing in Publication Data
Data available

ISBN: 978-0-19-275452-3

3 5 7 9 10 8 6 4 2

Printed in Great Britain
by Cox and Wyman Ltd, Reading Bershire

Paper used in the production of this book is a natural,
recyclable product made from wood grown in sustainable forests.
The manufacturing process conforms to the environmental
regulations of the country of origin.

*For Kyla*

# All manner of
# Super Spells
## and
# Powerful
# Potions

## Bespoke Broomsticks
## by the Bogle

### SPECIAL DISCOUNT RATE FOR
### EDUCATIONAL ESTABLISHMENTS

WE NUMBER AMONG OUR CLIENTS
THE ACADEMY OF ALCHEMISTS, AND
THE COLLEGE OF THE CRYSTAL BALL

### NO ORDER TOO PECULIAR

Wand maintenance undertaken

Leaky cauldrons repaired

Crystal balls re-energized

Difficult and disobedient
dragons retrained

# CONTENTS

# Summer School

'Has anyone seen my crystal ball?'

Midden, was rummaging about on the top of her desk in the Magic Factory in Starling Castle. She tucked her magic wand behind her ear and began to open the drawers of her desk one by one to search inside.

'I can't find it anywhere,' she said. 'And I really need it this morning.'

'Where did you have it last?' asked Corbie the Clever Crow, who was the most sensible member of Midden's team of helpers in the Magic Factory.

'If I knew that, I'd know where it is now,' said Midden quite crossly.

A large frog jumped out of one of the drawers as she opened it up. It landed on the floor and hopped away across the room.

'Oi! Come back here, you!' Midden called out. 'You've another three weeks to wait before that spell wears off and you turn back into a Handsome Prince.'

The Bogle, who was working on a broomstick in his corner by the fireplace, stuck out one of his four arms, scooped up the frog, and returned it gently to the desk drawer. Midden closed the drawer quickly and flopped down in her seat. 'Where could it be?' she said. 'I've looked everywhere.'

'Why do you need your crystal ball so urgently?' asked Cat-Astro-Phe, the cat from Ancient Egypt.

'Our Summer School begins today,' said Midden, 'and Doctor Distraction from the College of the Crystal Ball has asked me to take six of her students to help them with their magical studies. The lesson I'm going to teach is "Using a Crystal Ball Safely".'

'I didn't know that it was dangerous to use a crystal ball,' said the Bogle.

'It can be,' said Midden. 'That's why crystal balls are only issued under special licence from Magicians' Management Meetings. You have to be careful when using them. There are things better left unseen. And . . .' She broke off.

'And what?' asked the Bogle.

'Well,' said Midden, 'you have to make sure that you are in complete control of your crystal ball at all times. There are certain monstrous creatures who are always trying to find a way to break into our world and cause havoc. If you're careless, a Slimy Serpent or a Horrendous Hinkum might manage to get through.' She shuddered. 'They destroy everything they touch.'

Semolina the Shape Shifter changed from her usual puddingy shape and rolled herself into a ball. 'Would this do?' she asked Midden.

'Not really, Semolina,' said Midden. 'But thanks for trying.'

Growl the Gargoyle rapped on the outside of the window. 'Post!' he called out. 'A passing pigeon has just left a message from the College of the Crystal Ball.

It's the names of the students who are coming today, Midden.'

Cat went to the window and took the piece of paper from Growl. 'Your crystal ball is lying here on the window seat, Midden,' she mewed.

'Oh, I remember now,' said Midden. 'I was looking at it in the moonlight last night.' She picked up her crystal ball and blew on the surface. 'I wonder which students are coming for today's class.'

'Shall I read the names out to you from the list?' asked Cat.

'Yes, please,' said Midden, polishing her crystal ball with the end of her witch's cape.

Cat began to read out the names: 'Meera MacBeth, 'Zed the Zephyr—'

'He's the grandson of Nanny Northwind,' interrupted Midden. 'She said he might be one of my summer school students. He has trouble remembering things.'

'Goblin Garth,' Cat went on, 'Fairy Iola of Iona.' Cat paused. Her paws holding the piece of paper began to shake.

'That's only four,' said Midden. 'But I'm sure

4

Doctor Distraction said that there were six students who needed special tuition.'

Cat made a spluttering noise.

'Have you a fur ball caught in your throat?' Midden asked Cat anxiously.

Cat shook her head. She swallowed once or twice and began to cough.

'The last two students are . . .' Cat managed to gasp out the words, 'are . . . are . . . Boris and Cloris.'

'Boris and Cloris!' squawked Corbie. He flapped his wings in alarm, then flew up into the ceiling rafters and hid behind a beam.

'The terrible twins!' growled Growl. He stretched out one of his claws and slammed the window shut.

The Bogle clapped two of his hands over his ears and his other two hands over his eyes, something he only did if he was very, *very* stressed.

Semolina changed herself into a chair shape and walked over to the fireplace. 'I'll just sit quietly by the fire today, if you don't mind, Midden. I'd feel a lot safer there.'

'Well, I *do* mind,' said Midden. She looked at her team of helpers in the Magic Factory. 'Bogle, take your hands away from your eyes and ears. Corbie, I can see where you're hiding. Cat, stop coughing. Semolina, you may change yourself into any shape that suits you, but you can't stay inside the Magic Factory today. The students are due to arrive very soon. I really do need all of you in the courtyard of the castle to help me. And I've not forgotten about you, Growl.' Midden opened the window and looked outside. Growl's face was frightful, and he had shuffled as far along the outside windowsill as possible and was teetering right on the very edge. 'You don't have to join us in the courtyard, Growl,' said Midden, 'but will you please keep a close watch on everything that's happening during the lesson?'

*∗ ✳ ∗✳∗ ∗ ∗ ∗

Boris and Cloris were the two worst students in the College of the Crystal Ball. Every time they came to Starling Castle there was trouble. After a visit from the terrible twins, Jamie the Drawbridge Keeper had to mop up spills, mend broken windows, and replace tops of turrets. It usually took several days to calm down

Count Countalot who ran the Castle Café, and it was left to Midden to explain to the tourists and townspeople that children with magical powers didn't always behave better than children without them.

'I'm going to find Jamie,' said Midden, 'and ask him for six tables and chairs.' She put her crystal ball in a pocket of her cloak. 'As soon as Growl sees our students approaching I'd like the rest of you come down to assist me. Please,' Midden added, as she jammed on her witch's hat, jumped on her broomstick, and jetted out of the window of the Tallest Tower.

Midden hardly had time to help Jamie the Drawbridge Keeper set out the six tables and six chairs round the well in the middle of the courtyard before she heard Growl calling out, 'Six small broomsticks! Heading this way!'

Cat, Corbie, Semolina, and the Bogle hurried down the spiral staircase, through the Magic Factory shop, and along the secret passage. They opened the Hidden Door into the Deepest Dungeon and climbed the stairs out into the Castle Courtyard just as the six students brought their broomsticks in to land. Midden ticked their names off on her list.

'Meera MacBeth?' she called out.

Meera parked her broomstick and took her place at the front of the class.

'Zed the Zephyr?' said Midden.

Zed sat down beside Meera.

Goblin Garth and Fairy Iola of Iona sat in the second row while Boris and Cloris sat at the back.

'Have you all brought your crystal balls with you?' Midden asked.

The students nodded.

'And a notebook and pencil?'

'Oh, no!' said Zed. 'I've forgotten to bring a pencil.'

The Bogle stuck his hand down his right purple Bogle boot and found a pencil stub. He snapped his fingers. There was a crackle of magic and the pencil spun through the air and into Zed's hand.

'Thanks,' said Zed. 'I'm not very good at remembering things.'

'Neither am I,' the Bogle whispered in his ear. 'But it doesn't stop me doing magic.'

Midden rapped her wand on the side of the well.

'To begin with,' Midden began. 'I'm going to tell you a few "Dos" and "Don'ts" when using crystal balls. Even though your crystal balls have been set to low power, they are capable of doing some strong magic. So: *do* look after your crystal ball. *Do* treat it with respect.'

All the students wrote this down in their notebooks.

 'And,' said Midden, '*don't* play with your crystal ball or throw it about in case some scary monster appears in it. And if one does, *don't* try to deal with it on your own.

If you ever see any terrible thing inside your crystal ball, summon a senior magician immediately. These horrid beings are always trying to find an opening between the worlds to climb through to us.'

'*That* sounds very interesting,' Cloris whispered to Boris.

Boris nodded and winked at his sister.

'If any sounds come through your crystal ball,' Midden went on, '*do* get help. Beginners' use of crystal balls shouldn't involve the balls making noises. Your crystal balls should only be used for seeing the present, the immediate past, and the immediate future. For more complicated use you need a larger, more energized, ball.'

Meera put her hand up. 'What does it take to energize a crystal ball?'

'Dragon fire,' Midden answered her. 'Dragon Fire and Falling Water. And very occasionally you can use lightning, but only in extreme cases, as lightning makes the crystal ball unstable and unpredictable.'

'What about moonlight?' said Garth the Goblin.

'Neither moonlight nor sunlight give a crystal ball energy,' said Midden. 'But you can use both moonlight and sunlight for studying your crystal ball. Try to remember that the sun should be behind you, shining onto the ball—a bit like taking a photograph. In fact taking a photograph is very similar to what a crystal ball does. It takes a photograph, but not always in present time, and not of what you can see with your normal eyesight.'

'How do you spell photograph,' Zed whispered to the Bogle, writing furiously in his notebook.

'F-O-T-O-G-R-A-F,' said the Bogle.

'What about moonlight?' Goblin Garth asked Midden.

'Moonlight depends on the phases of the moon,' Midden answered. 'You will see different things by the light of the new moon, or the full moon, or the harvest moon.'

Fairy Iola put her hand up. 'What happens when someone with Second Sight uses a crystal ball?'

Midden searched her notes. 'We deal with Second Sight in lesson five,' she told Iola.

'Why not Lesson Two?' Cloris asked in a cheeky voice.

'That's right,' Boris, her twin, chimed in. 'After all, it is *second* sight. It should be lesson two, not lesson four.'

Corbie flew over to Boris. 'Pay attention!' he squawked in Boris's ear. Then he settled on Boris's shoulder and dug his claws in quite firmly.

Cat leapt into Cloris's lap. 'Sshhhhh!' she hissed and showed Cloris all her yellow teeth.

Boris and Cloris sat up straight and stopped giggling as Midden continued with the lesson.

'I think that's enough note taking for now,' said Midden after a while. 'We'll do some practical work next. Take out your crystal balls, please.'

The six students placed their crystal balls in front of them.

'As you all know,' said Midden, 'we must always use magic to try to help people, and a crystal ball can be very useful in doing this. Put your hands on either side of your crystal ball and concentrate very hard.'

'My crystal ball is showing me the laundry in Starling town,' said Meera. 'There are lots of clothes and sheets hanging outside to dry.'

Zed turned his crystal ball round and round. 'I see big black clouds blowing in from the mountains.'

'Why don't you two fly over to the laundry and let them know that it will rain this afternoon,' suggested Midden. 'You might even lend a hand to take in their washing.'

'Garth and I have both got a view of the Multi-Story School,' said Iola. 'The children are playing outside.'

'If you've both got the same view,' said Midden. 'Then it can mean that there's some trouble close by.'

'Oh!' gasped Iola. 'A bully is pushing a child on one of the swings. It's swinging far too high!'

'He's going to fall off!' said Garth.

'Onto your broomsticks then,' said Midden, 'and try to save him.'

Boris said, 'In my crystal ball there is a little girl whose boat has gone into the middle of the pond outside the castle wall.'

'Mine too,' said Cloris. 'She's crying.'

'Why don't you and your twin go and fetch the boat for her?' said Midden.

'That wasn't too bad,' said Midden, when the six students had flown out of the castle on their way to help the various people they had seen.

'There's still this afternoon,' said Cat. And her whiskers trembled the way they did when she could sense a catastrophe coming.

\*\* \*\*\*\*\*\* \*

'Broomsticks returning!' sang out Growl twenty minutes later.

Big drops of rain began to splash down as the students returned from their various missions. Cloris and Boris had given the girl her boat. They had also dipped in and out of the pond and splashed each other, but Midden decided to ignore their wet clothes.

Meera and Zed had brought in the washing for the town laundry. Zed had one sock round his neck and a pair of bloomers trailing from the back of his broomstick, but again Midden thought it better not to mention that.

Iola and Garth had flown right underneath the little boy as he tumbled from the swing. They had held hands and managed to catch him on their broomsticks before he crashed to the ground. Then they had picked up the bully and taken him to stand outside the door of

Professor Pernickety's office. He was head of the Multi-Story School.

'Well done, everyone,' said Midden. 'We'll go to the Castle Café and eat now.'

'It's crystal crêpes with scrumptious fillings, and moonlight meringues for afters.' The Bogle rubbed his tummy. 'Scrumptious Yumptious!'

While they were eating lunch the sky grew dark and the rain poured down. After lunch was over the Magic Factory Team stayed behind to help Count Countalot clear up. Midden noticed that the rain had stopped.

'Go outside now,' Midden told her six students, 'and give your broomsticks a good shake out. Then fly them about a bit to dry them off.'

While the other four students flew quietly up and down Cloris and Boris took out their crystal balls and began to throw them across the courtyard to each other.

'You shouldn't do that,' said Goblin Garth to Boris and Cloris. 'You're not supposed to fool around with a crystal ball.'

Meera nodded, and Iola said, 'Wasn't that in the list of "Dos" and "Don'ts"?'

Zed pulled his notebook from his pocket and opened it. 'You're right, Iola. Midden said, "*Do* treat your crystal ball with respect. *Don't* throw it about or play with it."'

'Who cares what Midden told us?' said Cloris rudely. She tossed her crystal ball high up into the sky.

'I can do what I like with my own crystal ball,' said Boris. And he threw his even higher than Cloris had thrown hers.

At that very moment a great jagged fork of lightning zigzagged down and zapped into the twins' crystal balls.

ZZZZZZap!!!!!!

There was a crash of thunder and smoke poured from the balls. They hung in mid-air without moving.

'Wha-at happened?' asked Zed.

'Let's have a look,' said Boris.

The students circled closer on their broomsticks.

'They're making a noise,' said Meera.

'And Midden said that could be dangerous,' said Garth.

A strange hissing sounded from inside Cloris's crystal ball.

A most peculiar grunting noise came from Boris's crystal ball.

Growl was having a quiet snooze.

It's quite exhausting being a gargoyle and having to keep look-out on the top of a high building day and night for hundreds and hundreds of years. So when he saw Midden and her students go into the Castle Café to eat lunch Growl thought that he too could have a little rest. After all, Midden had only asked him to keep an eye on everything that was happening during the lesson, not during their break time. Like most gargoyles, Growl had perfected the art of dozing with his eyes half open, and he was at a most interesting part of a dream when he heard the crack of a lightning bolt and the great rolling sound of thunder. He opened his eyes and saw Midden's six students hovering right beside two crystal balls which had begun to glow with a strange green light.

Then Growl heard the noises.

'Stay back!' he shouted, terrified.

Too late.

A huge Horrendous Hinkum exploded out of Boris's crystal ball and a long slithering Slimy Serpent blasted its way from Cloris's.

The children screamed. They desperately tried to dive out of the way.

But the Horrendous Hinkum stretched out its paws. It grabbed Meera and Zed in one, and Garth and Iola in the other.

The Slimy Serpent wrapped its tail around Cloris and its head around Boris.

With one paw the Horrendous Hinkum shook Meera and Zed until their eyes rolled about in their heads. With its other paw the Horrendous Hinkum shook Garth and Iola until their jaws rattled.

Then it opened its enormous mouth.

The Slimy Serpent coiled and rattled and slid and slithered around the courtyard. Boris and Cloris screamed and shouted and beat with their fists, but the Slimy Serpent only coiled itself tighter and tighter.

From the windowsill of the Tallest Tower Growl saw what was happening.

He stood up to his full height.

'MIDDEN!' he roared at the top of his voice.

Midden ran out of the Castle Café, followed by Semolina, Cat, Corbie, and the Bogle.

Semolina changed herself into a long piece of rope. She wrapped herself round the Horrendous Hinkum's ankles and tried to trip it up. The Horrendous Hinkum kicked out at Semolina so hard that she thought she was going to break in two. She was flung into the air and plunged down into the well.

Cat arched her back and spat and screeched. She clawed at the tail of the Slimy Serpent. But the Slimy Serpent lashed back at Cat and she was thrown across the courtyard.

Corbie flew up and tried to peck at the eyes of the

Horrendous Hinkum. But the Horrendous Hinkum flapped its wings and batted Corbie away.

The Bogle grabbed the Slimy Serpent round the neck with his four hands. But the Slimy Serpent wriggled free.

'Flippety Floo!' cried Midden. 'Flippety Floo! What can I do?' She pulled her wand from behind her ear and pointed it at the Slimy Serpent and the Horrendous Hinkum.

'Flippety Flop!' she shouted. 'Flippety Flop. Make them Stop!'

At once the Slimy Serpent stopped slithering. His head and tail uncurled and Cloris and Boris rolled free. The Horrendous Hinkum's paws unclenched and Meera and Zed and Garth and Iola began to tumble towards the ground but Growl caught them as they fell.

Midden stuck her wand back behind her ear and took her crystal ball from the pocket of her cape. She held it in both hands. Then she rubbed it very slowly round and round and said:

'*Three times now I rub this ball.*
*It's my intention to recall*
*These creatures to their own domain,*
*And, once at home, they must remain.*'

The students and the Magic Factory Team held their breath.

Would Midden's command work?

A thin red line of light came from Midden's crystal ball. It streamed out over the courtyard. It encircled the Slimy Serpent and rose up into the air towards the Horrendous Hinkum. It drew them both in and then turned, flowed back into Midden's crystal ball, and disappeared.

'The twins' crystal balls will have to be sent back to the College of the Crystal Ball to be repaired,' said Midden later when the students had gone home and the Magic Factory Team was relaxing round the fire. 'I'm sure Doctor Distraction will think of a suitable punishment for the twins for being so naughty.'

From outside the window Growl rolled his eyes and muttered, 'Let's hope Doctor Distraction doesn't decide that what the twins need are extra lessons at the Magic Factory Summer School.'

# A Magical Day in the Castle Café

Every day the five magicians in the Magic Factory—Midden the little witch who was in charge, Corbie the Clever Crow, the Bogle, Cat-Astro-Phe the Cat from Ancient Egypt, and Semolina the Shape Shifter—had breakfast delivered to them from the Café in Starling Castle.

Early each morning Jamie the Keeper of the Drawbridge would carry a large breakfast tray down to the Deepest Dungeon of the Castle, open the Hidden Door and walk along the Secret Passage to the Magic Factory Shop. He would go through to the back of the shop and climb up and up the spiral staircase of the Tallest Tower to the Magic Factory Workshops. On the tray was a plate with three slices of toast for Midden, an apple and some juicy berries for Corbie the Crow, a fresh fish for Cat, and a great big bowl of porridge for the Bogle. No one knew quite what Semolina the Shape Shifter ate—though it was noticed that whenever she went into the castle gardens beetles hid under leaves and small frogs hopped quickly away.

One summer morning, after Jamie the Drawbridge Keeper had left, Midden took the cover from the tray and the Magic Factory team sat down to eat their breakfast.

'Oh dear!' said Midden as she looked at her plate. 'That's very disappointing. I love my morning toast, but only if it's golden brown with the butter melting in little puddles.' Midden pointed at her toast. It was burned. To a crisp.

'I hope there's nothing wrong with my porridge,' said the Bogle. He leaned over and slurped a great mouthful of it.

'Yeechhh!' he screeched.

The porridge was lumpy and freezing cold.

'Not a single one of the Three Bears would eat any of this,' the Bogle moaned. 'Even Goldilocks herself wouldn't swallow a mouthful.'

Cat-Astro-Phe, the Cat from Ancient Egypt, sniffed at her fish. '*Phewwww!*' She held one paw over her nose. 'My fish has a *very* strong pong.'

Corbie the Crow flew down from where he had been chatting to Growl the Gargoyle who sat in the window. Growl sometimes helped out the Magic Factory team but he didn't eat breakfast, as he was made of stone. Corbie perched at his plate and pecked a piece from his apple. He spat it out at once. 'This apple wouldn't keep the doctor away. If I ate it I would need to call a doctor,' he cawed.

'I wonder what's gone wrong this morning,' said Midden. 'Count Countalot who runs the Café is usually very careful that every meal is perfectly prepared.'

'I could make a spell,' suggested the Bogle, who had only just begun to learn about magic and was always keen to try it out. He reached into his left purple Bogle boot for his bag of magic dust. 'It would just take me a couple of seconds to make breakfast for all of us.'

'No,' said Midden.

'Just one tiny spell,' pleaded the Bogle, 'to heat up my porridge.'

'No,' said Midden again. 'That would be wasting good magic. I'll walk along to the Castle Café and find out what has happened.' The little witch picked up the breakfast tray. 'Wait here,' she told the rest of the team.

'Hurry up,' said the Bogle. His tummy made a rumbling sound. 'I'm hungry.'

Midden went down the spiral staircase of the Tallest Tower, through the Magic Factory Shop and along the Secret Passage. She opened the Hidden Door into the Deepest Dungeon and climbed the steps out into the courtyard of Starling Castle. From there she made her way to the Castle Café.

Inside the Castle Café the manager, Count Countalot, was tearing his hair out. Everything on the food counter was in a mess. There was macaroni mixed in with muesli, peas among the pancakes, and carrots in the custard.

'Goodness me!' said Midden. 'This does look a bit of a disaster. What's the problem?' she asked Count Countalot.

'The cook is on holiday,' Count Countalot told Midden. 'Yesterday the assistant cook took ill. This morning the assistant to the assistant cook telephoned me to say that her boy has Strange Spots and she can't possibly come to work today.

Then the counter server and the dish-washer phoned to say that they had Strange Spots too. Now I'm trying to serve at the counter, take the money at the till, clear the tables, wash the dishes, and cook all the food. There's a whole coach-load of visitors due to arrive at lunchtime and I just can't cope. What am I to do?'

Midden looked round the Café. She had an idea. 'I could help,' she said.

'Could you?' asked Count Countalot. 'I'd be so grateful.'

'We *all* will,' said Midden. 'The whole Magic Factory team.'

'Including the Bogle?' asked Count Countalot, becoming a little pale.

'The Bogle is much more careful now,' Midden said reassuringly. 'He doesn't break things. Well, not as often as he used to,' she added under her breath. And off she went to the Magic Factory to tell her team that they were on duty in the Castle Café until the assistant to the assistant cook's son and the rest of the staff stopped having Strange Spots.

**\* \* \*\*\*\* \* \***

By the time the visitors arrived at the Café of Starling Castle the Magic Factory team was in place and knew what they had to do.

Count Countalot was in charge of clearing tables. Corbie was to fly backwards and forwards between the kitchen and the counter with the food orders. Cat was taking the money at the till. Midden was cooking in the kitchen, and the Bogle, who had four arms, was serving at the counter and washing the dishes at the same time.

'Try not to frighten anybody,' Midden warned her team of magicians. 'The people in Starling Castle and the town are quite used to us. But it's not the same with visitors, especially the adults. They don't always understand that lots of different types of creatures live on the earth.'

'But this is a castle,' said Cat. 'And Starling Castle is a very, very old castle. People should expect to see weird things.'

'Not *that* weird.' Midden tucked the Bogle's two extra arms under the counter. 'I'll put a basin under there for you, Bogle. Then you can wash the dishes and cutlery with your two lower hands and use your two top

ones to serve at the counter.
Try to keep those two extra
ones out of sight. And
no magic,' she told
him. 'Promise?'

The Bogle nod-
ded. But behind his
back he crossed the
fingers on three of his
four hands.

*∗ ∗*∗*∗*∗ ∗ *

The tour bus arrived and all
the people crowded into the Café.

Midden peeked out from the kitchen. She gave a
groan. A huge line of customers was waiting to be
served.

The people in the queue gave their orders for their
food. Midden cooked. Count Countalot cleared. The
Bogle served (sometimes using his extra arms when he
thought no one was looking). But still the queue of
people moved very slowly.

If I did some magic, thought the Bogle, I could

hurry things along a bit. He glanced through the hatch to the kitchen. Midden was busy frying eggs and grilling toast. A tiny spell wouldn't do any harm.

Would it?

Well, maybe not a spell as such.

Maybe just a teensy amount of the magic dust that he always kept in a little bag in his boot for situations like this.

And he wouldn't do a spell. Only make a wish.

A strong wish.

The Bogle pulled his Bogle bag from the inside of his left purple Bogle boot. He opened it up and took out a small amount of magic dust. He sprinkled it very lightly on the clean stacked dishes and cutlery and whispered quietly:

> 'Fork, knife, plate, cup
> Make the people eat up!'

A few minutes later a badly behaved boy called George sat down at a nearby table with his mum and his little sister in her buggy.

'I don't like that,' said Bad George pointing to the lovely stew his mum had placed in front of him.

'At least eat *some* of it, George.' His mum bent down to lift the baby from the buggy and put her in the high chair.

'I said I don't like it,' snapped Bad George.

Oh no! thought his mum. George is going to be badly behaved in public again. 'At least try it,' she coaxed him.

'I don't want to try it,' said Bad George. 'I don't like it!'

'Well, I don't like you either,' said his dinner plate.

'Whaaaat?' Bad George stared at his plate in amazement.

'You heard me,' said his dinner plate. 'But just in

case you didn't, I'll say it louder.' The plate took a deep breath and shouted at the top of its voice. 'I DON'T LIKE YOU!'

George's mum turned round and glared at him. 'That is *so* impolite,' she said.

'But I didn't say it,' said Bad George.

'I heard you say it, George,' said his mum.

'It was my plate that said it,' said Bad George. 'It spoke to me.'

'Don't tell fibs,' said his mum. She turned away to spoon some goo into the baby's mouth.

'Better eat your food up quickly,' the plate said quietly. 'Else I'll cause lots more trouble.'

'I don't believe you,' sneered Bad George. 'What could you do? You're only a plate.'

'Well, this for starters.' And the plate blew a loud raspberry sound.

Everybody nearby began to laugh at George for making such a babyish noise.

'Really, George!' said his mum. 'I won't put up with that kind of behaviour when we are eating out.'

'But I didn't do it,' said Bad George.

'If you don't stop fibbing,' his mum replied, 'I'm not

going to buy any pudding.'

'But . . . but . . . but . . .' said Bad George.

'I'd eat up my dinner if I were you,' George's plate told him. 'I will make *much* worse noises than that if you don't.'

\*\* \*\*\*\*\* \*\* \*

Over in the corner, a very large man was about to eat his lunch. On his plate he had put a small fish, some vegetables, and heaps and heaps and heaps of chips.

'You know the doctor said you shouldn't eat fried foods,' his wife said anxiously. She put her own plate on the table and went to fetch some water.

The very large man picked up his knife and fork. 'It doesn't really matter what you eat,' he called after his wife.

The knife twisted in his hand and spun round to face him. 'Of course it does,' the knife said severely. 'Eating too much junk food is not good for you. Everybody knows that. Though you wouldn't think so. Years and years I've been in the Castle Café and the amount of junk food I've watched people eat you wouldn't believe.'

The fork in the man's other hand leaned over. 'Tell me about it, ducks,' it called across to the knife. 'And they expect us to touch it too! Oooohhhh!' The fork shivered. 'I tell you, I don't like putting a single prong of mine into some of the stuff they shove into their mouths.'

The man's wife came back with the two glasses of water.

'I've got talking cutlery,' he told her.

'Oh, don't be silly,' said his wife.

'No really. This knife and fork.' He held them up. 'They were having a conversation with each other. And they were speaking to me too.'

'It's a pity you didn't hear me speaking to you last night,' his wife replied. 'Especially when I was telling you not to drink any more of those malt whisky samples on the distillery tour. If you had listened to me then, you might not be hearing talking cutlery now.'

'It must be some kind of animated hologram type thing,' said the man. 'Part of the Castle entertainment.'

'Whatever you say, dear.' His wife began to eat her lunch.

37

The very large man began to eat *his* lunch. He wanted to eat six chips in one go. But when he tried to spear them, his fork bent sideways and scooped up some vegetables instead. The man had put them in his mouth before he realized what had happened.

'Well done, you!' the knife cried out to the fork. 'He never saw that coming.'

'I do my best,' the fork said modestly.

'Uuulmp,' said the very large man, his mouth full of carrots, peas, and broccoli.

'Eat your vegetables all up now like a good boy,' the knife whispered to him encouragingly.

'Uuuulmp,' said the man, trying to swallow the last piece of broccoli.

At a table near the door a frail old lady was with her granddaughter. The little girl's name was Arabella. Everyone knew her as Rude Arabella. This was because she was a very rude girl. Her gran was quite tired and worn out with looking after her.

Arabella grabbed her spoon and began to slurp her chocolate ice cream in the most disgusting manner.

'Your table manners are appalling,' said the ice cream bowl.

'Couldn't agree more,'said the spoon. 'Did you see the way she just grabbed me and began gobbling her food?'

'The dishes are speaking to me,' Rude Arabella told her gran.

'Of course they are,' said her gran in a tired voice.

Rude Arabella's gran had decided a long time ago that it was much easier to agree with whatever Rude Arabella said. That way she didn't get so many headaches and it meant she wasn't quite so exhausted after a day in Arabella's company.

'No, they really did.' Rude Arabella spoke crossly. 'And they were very cheeky to me.'

'That wasn't cheek,' said the spoon. 'That was the truth. Grab and gobble. That's what you did. Grab and gobble.'

'Shockingly rude,' agreed the ice cream bowl.

'They're doing it again,' said Rude Arabella.

'That's nice, dear,' said her gran.

Rude Arabella made a very rude face behind her gran's back. So rude that it's difficult to describe. It involved screwing up her eyes, pulling her mouth, sticking out her tongue, and twisting her nose sideways.

'Now you've gone too far!' Arabella's ice cream bowl exclaimed. 'I won't stand for any more of this. Not for a single second.'

Rude Arabella folded her arms. 'So what are you going to do about it?' she demanded.

'This,' said the ice cream bowl. It tipped itself up and

Rude Arabella's chocolate ice cream slopped onto her lap. There was none left in the dish for her to eat and her clothes were wet through.

'I want to go home and lie down,' wailed Rude Arabella.

'Oh . . . good,' said her gran. She stood up at once. Usually it was she who felt the need to go home and lie down after an hour with Arabella.

As she left the Castle Café, Rude Arabella's gran put a large amount of money into the staff tip jar on the counter. Perhaps this afternoon if Arabella had a little nap, she could put her feet up and have some peace to read a book for an hour or so.

On her way out of the café Bad George's mum also left some coins in the glass dish on the counter. 'Make sure the cook gets that,' she said. 'That's the first time George has eaten a whole meal without making a huge fuss.'

The very large man's wife added her own tip to the dish. 'Having a meal here is the best thing that's happened to me in a long time,' she told Count Countalot. 'I've been so worried about my husband's health. He's always promising to eat less fatty food and more greens but today he actually did it. There's something magical about this Castle Café.'

Count Countalot looked across at the Bogle. One of the Bogle's extra arms had drifted out from under the counter. He was using it to scratch behind his ear.

'I can't think what you mean,' said Count Countalot.

# Wailing William

Crash! The great door of Starling Castle swung open with a bang.

'Who's there?' asked Jamie the Drawbridge Keeper.

'No body,' came the whispered reply.

Jamie felt a cold breeze brush past his face. 'Oh, it's you, William,' he said.

'Yes,' the whisper came again. 'It's only me.'

Wailing William, the ghost of Starling Castle, slowly materialized. He wore a tunic and trousers, big boots, and a cloak.

Long, long ago Wailing William had been a nobleman and had lived in the Castle. He was a cousin, twice removed, of the more famous Sir William

Wallace. The famous Sir William Wallace had lots of things named after him, like a monument, a hill, and a tea room. Wailing William didn't have anything named after him, but the people in Starling town and castle thought he was a great ghost.

'What's the matter?' asked Jamie.

'I'm feeling sad.'

'Fancy a cup of tea?'

'Just a half cup,' Wailing William replied very softly.

'Sit down and I'll put the kettle on.' Jamie stirred the coals in the fire with a poker. 'Summer's almost here and we're expecting loads of visitors. That should cheer you up. You're always happier when the tourists come, aren't you?'

Jamie knew that Wailing William enjoyed the tourist season. From the beginning of summer until the end of autumn, coach-loads of boys and girls, mums and dads, aunts and uncles, and grannies and grandpas would arrive in Starling Castle every day. These visitors would eat in the Castle Café and buy things, including postcards, from the Castle shop. One of the most popular postcards showed Wailing William walking on the Castle battlements. It was just a drawing, because, of course, you can't take a photograph of a real ghost.

Wailing William worked hard at his job of being a ghost. He hid behind pillars and sighed loudly. He crept into the Great Hall and blew on the fire in the fireplace so that the flames would leap up even when there was no wind. He stamped through the rooms in the Castle crying and moaning. One of his favourite places was the old well in the middle of the courtyard. He would sit in there quite happily for hours making sobbing sounds which carried all the way up to the Tallest Tower and echoed off the rooftops of Starling Castle. But his most important job, his very special event, when he gave his all-time best performance, was the seasonal Ghost Walk. During the summer months, at the stroke of midnight, William would appear on the battlements and let out the most unearthly wails.

Wailing William's wails were so loud that they could be heard as far south as the Tower of London and as far north as the High Highlands. The Beefeaters in the Tower of London had once sent a message telling William his wailing was the most creepy sound they'd ever heard. They said he was much more spooky than the ghosts of the two little princes in the Tower, who giggled and laughed as they ran about playing. Nanny Northwind and Goodwife MacGumboil, two old witches who lived far to the north in the High Highlands of Scotland both said that they loved to hear Wailing William wailing every summer night. He was so reliable that they set their clocks by him.

Very occasionally when people were visiting Starling Castle they would say that it couldn't be a real ghost that was making those noises. They would say that it was only a recording and look around for hidden microphones. When that happened, Wailing William would appear, wave at them, and then vanish through

a wall. Once, two very cheeky children, Bad George and Rude Arabella, came to visit the Castle. They said they didn't think ghosts existed at all. They said that they thought that the Starling Castle ghost was only a computer generated hologram.

Wailing William hadn't been the least bit annoyed when he heard that. He waited until Bad George was licking an ice lolly, and then had gently taken it from his hand and eaten it himself right in front of Bad George. And when Rude Arabella had said she didn't believe in ghosts, Wailing William had lifted her right up into the air and set her down on the roof of the Great Hall. Jamie the Drawbridge Keeper had to call three fire engines and a battalion of soldiers to get her down again.

Now, Jamie the Drawbridge Keeper didn't like to see Wailing William looking so sad so he reminded his friend about how everyone loved his special Ghost Walk.

'I won't be going a-haunting this year,' Wailing William whispered.

'What!' said Jamie. 'Not go a-haunting! But you're a ghost. You *must* go a-haunting.'

'I can't do it,' said Wailing William.

48

'Can't do it!' Jamie repeated. 'You can't *can't* do it. You're the Castle Ghost. Who else would sigh in the stables and weep behind the wainscot?'

'Not me,' said Wailing William.

'But we need you to howl in the Great Hall, groan in the gardens, and wail along the walls at midnight.'

'I'm not able to any more,' said Wailing William.

'But why ever not?' Jamie asked him.

'I can't talk about it,' sighed Wailing William. 'It's too embarrassing.' He drank the rest of his tea and drifted off through the wall in the direction of the castle gardens.

\*\* \* \*\*\* \* \*

Without even stopping to rinse out the teacups Jamie got up and hurried over the drawbridge into Starling Castle. As he passed the well in the courtyard he heard a most peculiar sound. 'A frog must have fallen in the well,' he said aloud. 'I'll need to help it out of there when I get a minute.' Jamie went quickly on down to the Deepest Dungeon of the Castle. Once there he opened a Hidden Door and walked along a Secret Passage until he reached the Magic Factory shop. At the back of the shop was a spiral staircase that led to the top of the Tallest Tower and the Magic Factory workshops.

'We have an emergency,' Jamie told Midden, the little witch who was in charge of the Magic Factory in Starling Castle.

'What's an Emer Genie?' asked the Bogle. He was a big hairy beastie with four arms, and one of the Magic Factory Team. 'I've heard of Jeanie with the Light Brown Hair,' the Bogle went on, 'and the Genie of Aladdin's Lamp, but I've never heard of an Emer Genie.'

'An E-M-E-R-G-E-N-C-Y,' said Semolina the Shape Shifter, spelling out the word for the Bogle. 'It means a serious situation. Something that needs dealing with at once.' She changed slowly from her normal puddingy shape into a question mark. 'What's wrong?' she asked Jamie the Drawbridge Keeper.

'It's Wailing William,' said Jamie. 'He says he's not going a-haunting this year.'

Corbie, the crow who was the cleverest member of the Magic Factory Team, had also been listening to what Jamie was saying. 'That *is* an emergency,' he cawed loudly. 'If Wailing William doesn't appear this summer, then Starling Castle could be ruined.'

'Very purr-ceptive of you,' purred Cat-Astro-Phe, the cat from Ancient Egypt. 'But I'd say it would be more of a *catastrophe*. The leaflets advertising Starling Castle's Ghost Walk have been printed and sent out and hundreds of tickets have been sold already. If William doesn't appear the tourists will feel cheated and ask for their money back.'

'You can't have a Ghost Walk without a ghost walking,' said Growl the Gargoyle from his place on the windowsill.

'We need to talk to Wailing William,' said Midden. 'Do you know where he is now?'

'He went off in the direction of the castle gardens.'

Growl the Gargoyle swivelled round and looked down into the castle gardens. Growl had very keen eyesight and he spotted Wailing William at once. 'I see him,' he told the others, 'he's at the far end of the garden hiding behind one of the stone urns.'

'I'll go and speak to him,' said Midden. She snapped her fingers and her broomstick, which she had left leaning against her desk, rose up and hovered beside her. Midden tucked her wand behind her

ear. Then she jammed on her witch's hat, jumped on her broomstick, and jetted out of the window of the Tallest Tower. As she flew over the Castle courtyard Midden heard an odd noise from the well. Don't tell me that one of those Handsome Princes has been changed into a frog again, she thought as she turned her broomstick towards the castle gardens.

Midden bumped her broomstick onto the ground close to where Wailing William was standing.

'I hear you're not feeling very well,' Midden said gently. 'What's the matter?'

'Can't you tell?' whispered William. 'It's really awful.'

Midden looked at William. 'You look good to me,' she said. 'Your boots are shiny and your cloak is swirly. You look ghostly, but not too scary for little children.'

'Listen,' said Wailing William very softly.

'Actually, William,' said Midden, 'I can't really hear you. Could you speak up a bit, please?'

'No,' whispered Wailing William. 'I can't. That's what's wrong. I've lost my voice.'

'You've lost your voice!' Midden repeated.

Wailing William nodded, and two big tears slid out of his eyes and ran down his cheeks. 'I woke up this morning and it was gone. When I speak only a whisper comes out. When I try to wail I can only manage a muffled groan or a little sob. It's a disaster. The Ghost Walk leaflets advertise me as Wailing William. People set their clocks by my especially loud midnight wail. The Beefeaters in the Tower of London, Nanny Northwind and Goodwife MacGumboil in the Highlands, and all the tourists listen out for me. How can I be Wailing William if I can't wail?'

\*\* \*\*\*\*\*\*\* \* \*

'We'll have to use some very special magic for Wailing William,' Midden declared.

Wailing William sat by the fireplace in the Magic Factory while Jamie the Drawbridge Keeper and the members of the Magic Factory Team discussed how they could help him start to wail again.

'It's going to take something c-awfully strong,'

cawed Corbie, nodding his head in agreement with Midden.

'Perhaps I could shape shift myself into looking like William?' suggested Semolina. She put out her arms and stretched herself as high as she could until her head touched the roof.

'Now you just look like a very tall pencil,' said Growl.

Semolina gave herself a shake and went back to her normal puddingy shape. 'It's no good,' she said. 'I can't make myself see-through or disappear.'

'We could advertise for another ghost to come and give Wailing William a holiday,' said Cat.

'That's a good idea,' said Midden. 'But the leaflets for the Ghost Walk are printed, and they say that the Castle Ghost is Wailing William.'

'We could use magic dust,' said the Bogle. He shoved one of his four hands down the inside of his left Bogle boot and brought out the little bag where he kept his sparkly magic dust. 'I've got some left in my Bogle bag.'

'Magic dust may not be strong enough on its own,' Midden reminded the Bogle. 'Let's see if there is anything suitable already made up in our store.' She went to the row of shelves beside the fireplace and bent down to the one marked W. She rummaged among the boxes and jars. '"Walking Stick that takes owner for nice walk", "Wart powder—grow your own to any size, any colour", "Womble Finder", "Jumping Beans" . . . They shouldn't be there.' Midden tossed the box of Jumping Beans onto a shelf marked F. 'We need to tidy the store shelves more often.' She straightened up. 'There's nothing here for someone who has lost their wail.'

Cat and Corbie had been flicking through the books of magic that were lying around on the workshop tables. 'Nothing in any of these either,' they said.

'I'll have a look among the older books of spells and power-ful potions that we keep on the high shelves,' said Midden.

Semolina the Shape Shifter turned herself into a long ladder and Midden climbed up to the very top. She gathered up a huge pile of magic books and then staggered back down and dumped them on the big worktable. A great cloud of dust billowed into the air.

'Here's one!' said Semolina opening the first book. 'It's a spell that stops people from sitting down. If you put that spell on William then he would have to walk.'

'But that wouldn't make him wail,' said Midden. 'And anyway that spell only lasts a short time. What would we do when it wore off?'

'I've got one!' said the Bogle. He read from another book. 'It's a very short spell and it works right away. A few words, a wave from Midden's magic wand and William will make sounds again.'

'OK,' said Midden. She pulled her wand from behind her ear. 'You say the words, Bogle.'

The Bogle chanted aloud:

> *'Make a sound*
> *That is found*
> *Close to the ground.'*

Midden pointed her magic wand at William.
**Zippity Zap!!!**

There was a pause.

Wailing William opened his mouth. A long mournful howl echoed round the room.

'He sounds like a dog howling,' said Midden. She snatched the book from the Bogle's hand and read it herself.

> 'Make a sound
> Like a hound
> That is found
> Close to the ground.'

'Ooops, sorry,' said the Bogle.

'Don't worry, William,' said Midden. 'We'll try again.'

'**Owww. Owww. Owwwwwwwww!**' William howled mournfully.

'Why don't we just change his name to Howling Horace?' suggested Cat.

'There already is a Howling Horace and he haunts Hampton Court,' said Midden. 'And he's very huffy. If he heard that William was howling instead of wailing he'd probably not speak to us for at least a hundred years.'

'We could try this potion,' said Corbie. He read from

a different magic book. 'For lots of choice in a voice, chop up one raggle-snaggle rumbleweed, mix with two parts snizzle-drizzle, and boil for three minutes. Allow to cool before drinking.'

'We've got some snizzle-drizzle,' said Cat. She reached out a dainty paw and picked up a little bottle full of pale green liquid.

'And there's some rumbleweed in the castle gardens,' said Jamie. 'I'll go and fetch it.'

On his way to the castle gardens to get the raggle-snaggle rumbleweed Jamie noticed that the noise from the well in the courtyard was louder than ever. He peered down into the well, but he couldn't see any frogs. As he turned away he thought he heard a voice call out 'Help!'

When Jamie brought the raggle-snaggle rumbleweed to Midden he mentioned the noise in the well in the courtyard.

'I heard it too,' said Midden. 'It's probably another Handsome Prince who's been changed into a frog. They always come here for me to lift the spell. The well is a good place for him to wait. It's cool and dark and frogs like it there.'

'I was sitting down the well yesterday myself,' barked Wailing William. 'And I didn't see any frogs.'

'Let's get you sorted out first,' said Midden. 'Then I'll take a look in the well.'

Using his four hands, the Bogle chopped the raggle-snaggle rumbleweed. Corbie gathered it up and put it in a bowl. Cat poured in the right amount of snizzle-drizzle and Semolina changed herself into a beater and mixed the mixture thoroughly. Green smoke bubbled from the potion as Midden stirred it into the cauldron on the fire. When it had cooled, Midden poured some out and Wailing William drank it down.

Everyone waited.

William opened his mouth.

'**OINK!**'

'Pardon?' said Midden

'**HEE-HAW! HEE-HAW!**' brayed William.

'Try again,' said Semolina encouragingly.

'**COCK-A-DOODLE DOOOOOOOOOOOO!!!!!!!**' William screeched.

'Lots of choice in a voice?' Midden said, looking at Corbie. 'That potion has given William *animal* voices.'

'**QUACK!**' said William.

'We've made things worse, not better,' said Midden.

'**MOO! MOO!**' William nodded his head.

'It's like MacDonald's farm in here, not the Magic Factory,' said Jamie the Drawbridge Keeper.

'**BAAA!**' bleated William.

\*\* \* \*\* \*\* \* \*

Growl the Gargoyle could hear the cries for help from the well in the Castle courtyard getting louder and louder. 'Perhaps you should take a break from curing William,' he called to Midden from the window. 'It sounds as though that Handsome Prince is in a panic.'

Midden's ears were beginning to ache with all William's mooing and barking and she was quite glad to do something else. She grabbed her broomstick and flew out of the window.

Two minutes later she was back holding something in her hands.

'William,' she said. 'Open your mouth.'

When William opened his mouth, Midden opened her hands and put something carefully inside.

'Now swallow,' Midden instructed William.

William gulped and then swallowed.

'What was that?' William asked the little witch.

'Your voice,' said Midden. 'I should have listened more carefully when you told me you had lost it. It was lying at the bottom of the well. You must have mislaid it when you were sitting down there yesterday.'

'Thank you, Midden,' smiled William, using his own voice again. 'Thank **you-ooo-ooo-ooo-ooooooo-oooooooooo!**'

# Midden's Midsummer Barbecue

'Are you sure that you want to be the one to go and ask Snap to do this for us?'

It was Midsummer's Day and Midden the little witch was standing in the Magic Factory talking to Corbie the Clever Crow. 'Remember, one has to be very, very polite when talking to a dragon,' she said.

'I remember,' said Corbie.

'And you must address him by his proper title, which is *Sir* Snap the Dragon,' Midden went on. 'Dragons like to be praised.'

'I know that,' said Corbie.

'And because we're asking him to do us a favour, be sure to say "please".'

'I will,' said Corbie.

'In fact, say "please" several times,' added Midden.

'Midden!' squawked Corbie. 'I see Snap quite frequently when I fly through the swamp collecting herbs and plants for our spells and potions. I know how to treat dragons.'

'Just remember one can never trust a dragon,' said Midden. 'They are extremely short tempered creatures and very unpredictable.'

'Snap is different,' said Corbie. 'I think he might be a bit lonely out there all on his own. There isn't another dragon for a hundred miles or more. There's Nessie up in Loch Ness but she's so busy hiding from the tourists that she hardly ever gets out and about. Sometimes I think Snap looks forward to seeing me. When I'm flying backwards and forwards collecting ingredients for the Magic Factory he often waves a wing or calls out a greeting.'

'Well, if you're certain he won't snap at you . . . ' said Midden.

'Snap? Snap at *me*? No way!' said Corbie sounding very confident.

But deep down in his feathered chest Corbie *was* a little nervous. He recalled something that had happened yesterday when he'd been flying over the swamp. Snap had waved one of his wings in what Corbie took to be a jolly greeting—but the dragon had caught Corbie a clout round the back of his head. And last week, Snap had shouted 'Hello!' burping an enormous blast of hot air that had singed Corbie's claws. Then there was the time when Corbie hadn't been paying attention and

had found himself dangerous-
ly close to Snap's large teeth.
The Clever Crow had had to
flap his wings furiously to
escape, losing a few feathers in
the process.

However, Corbie decided to put all those mishaps
down to Snap being careless, and himself not getting
out of the way fast enough. 'He doesn't come out of the
swamp very often,' Corbie told Midden. 'He's quite a
shy dragon.'

'Well, you see if you can persuade him,' said
Midden. 'When he hears that we're having our
Midsummer's Day Barbecue this afternoon and we're
looking to him to help us light the coals he might
fly over to the castle gardens and oblige.'

'Tell Snap we're relying on him.' Growl the
Gargoyle spoke quietly to Corbie as the Crow stood
on the windowsill of the Tallest Tower of Starling
Castle getting ready for take-off. 'Otherwise everyone
will be eating half-cooked hamburgers and cold corn-
on-the-cob.'

'I know,' Corbie whispered back. 'Midden's good at

magic but barbecue cooking isn't one of her special skills. I'll do my best.'

Corbie gave a little skip and a hop, spread his wings, and flew off in the direction of the swamp.

Corbie had to search for a few hours before he found Snap. The dragon was sitting under a tree cleaning his teeth with his claws. He looked cross.

'Your Highness,' Corbie called out as he came in to land a little way off. 'O Excellency, Your Lordship, Right Honourable, Most Gracious and Great Dragon,' he went on, keeping himself well out of fire-blasting range. 'Most Noble and Mighty Warrior whom Kings tremble before and brave Knights run away from. May I ask you for a favour?'

'Buzz off, crow,' snapped Snap. 'Can't you see I'm busy?'

Corbie blinked. Perhaps he hadn't praised Snap enough?

'O amazing creature,' proclaimed Corbie, 'whose scales shine in the sun, whose wings are wondrous, whose tail is terrifying, whose eyes are . . . er . . . eye-

catching, whose claws—' Corbie broke off as he noticed the very old and smelly piece of food that Snap had just picked out of his teeth with one of his claws. Corbie rattled out his last sentence. 'I'd like to ask you if you'd be good enough to come and light up the Magic Factory's Midsummer Barbecue this afternoon and help cook the food.'

'No,' said Snap.

Drat! thought Corbie. I forgot to say 'please'.

'Please,' Corbie said quickly, 'pretty please. I beg you. I implore, beseech, entreat, and urge you to reconsider. If you could see your way clear to, if you wouldn't mind, if it wasn't too much trouble, if you might oblige us, we would be eternally grateful, and I'd go humbly down on one knee—'

'I didn't know that birds had knees,' Snap interrupted Corbie in full flow.

'What?' said Corbie.

'Birds,' repeated Snap. 'I didn't realize they had knees.'

'That's not the point,' said Corbie, forgetting to be clever and foolishly stepping closer to the dragon. 'It was to indicate my frame of mind. I meant that if I had a knee, I would go down on it, and indeed both, if you wanted me to. What I'm trying to say is, that we are begging you to come and light our barbecue.'

'Well, I'm not going to,' said Snap. 'I don't really like coming out of my Swamp. The answer's "no", so there.'

'But we really do need you, Snap. Midden likes to do the Midsummer Barbecue but she never gets the fire going properly and everyone is so looking forward to lovely toasted treats this afternoon.'

Snap grinned and Corbie saw all of his jagged yellow teeth. 'Me too,' said the dragon. 'I think I might have toasted crow.' And he let  a long lick of fire spiral out of his mouth.

Corbie screeched, leapt back, and scrambled into the air to take refuge in a high tree branch.

'I'm going for a sleep,' Snap said as he got up. 'And no one had better disturb me,' he added as he lumbered off in the direction of his cave.

\* \* \* \* \* \* \*

'That dragon's not called Snap for nothing,' said Midden when Corbie reported back to the Magic Factory. 'Thanks for trying, Corbie, but I'll just have to make sure the barbecue coals are properly lit myself.'

The members of the Magic Factory team exchanged glances. Midden wasn't the best of cooks. She was always letting her cauldron boil over and put the fire out.

'Count Countalot could help,' Semolina the Shape Shifter suggested diplomatically. 'He loves doing that sort of thing.'

'No,' said Midden firmly. 'Count Countalot works very hard and prepares the food for our special celebrations. He's entitled to at least one day off every year.'

'How about some magic?' said the Bogle.

'I've told you before, Bogle,' said Midden, 'that magic's not there to make us lazy. I'll manage, don't you worry.'

'But we do. We do worry,' Cat hissed quietly as Midden went off down the spiral staircase to set up her barbecue.

At the bottom of the spiral staircase of the Tallest Tower was the Magic Factory Shop. As Midden went through the shop to get to the Secret Passage that led to the main part of the castle she paused for a minute. She had told the Bogle that magic must not be used to encourage laziness, but she knew that sometimes she had a problem getting the barbecue to light properly.

Midden went behind the shop counter and picked up a Crackle Pop. She read the instructions.

*Add to anything to make it Crackle and Pop!*

That's quite simple, she thought. It would help start off the barbecue. Magicians were supposed to do magic to help others, Midden thought, but that didn't mean that you couldn't help yourself occasionally.

It wasn't often that she used tricks or spells or potions for her own benefit, but this time Midden felt she should. Otherwise the barbecue might not be a success. She put a dozen Crackle Pops in a pocket of her witch's cape. Then she went out of the shop and along the Secret Passage. She opened the Hidden Door into the Darkest Dungeon and climbed up the stairs and made her way to the castle gardens.

Jamie the Drawbridge Keeper was already putting out the big barbecue stand and grill pan. Jamie also knew that Midden wasn't good at making her barbecue catch fire, so he'd brought some extra strength firelighters and now he placed these under the coals where they couldn't be seen.

'That ought to do it,' he said.

Midden waited until Jamie's back was turned. Then she took the twelve Crackle Pops from inside her cape and scattered them over the top of the coals.

'That ought to do it,' said the little witch.

Meanwhile, back in the Magic Factory workshop at the top of the Tallest Tower, Semolina and Cat were

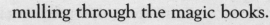

mulling through the magic books.

'Here's a recipe that might help,' said Cat. 'It was used in ancient times to light the great lighthouse at Alexandria. It's a potion that you add to whatever fuel you are using and it makes the fire burn more brightly.'

'And we've got all the ingredients right here,' said Semolina leaning over Cat's shoulder to read the page. '*To make Fizzing Fire, take red ragwort and blazing bindweed. Mix together over a hot flame until they melt.*'

Semolina lit the burner flame on the workbench while Cat found the ingredients on the shelves of the Magic Factory. Then they both took turns at stirring the mixture until it became a smooth liquid.

'It's ready,' said Semolina. 'We can go down and offer to help and find a way to slip the stuff on to the fire.'

'That ought to do it,' said Cat, pouring the potion into a small bottle.

\*\* \*\*\*\*\*\*\* \* \*

Corbie was out on the windowsill chatting to Growl.

'What can we do?' the Clever Crow asked the Gargoyle.

'There's old, old magic,' said Growl. 'Being made of stone, I have some of it inside me. Fire began in Stone Age times. There are some words I know, from when I was just a lump of stone that a cave man used to sit on, before I was fashioned into a gargoyle.'

'Tell me them,' said Crow.

'All right,' said Growl, 'but use them gently.'

Corbie nodded in agreement. 'We only need a little bit of fire,' he said, 'to get the barbecue going.'

> '*Wind blow*
> *Flames flow*
> *Fire glow*,' Growl chanted.

Repeating these words very softly Corbie flew up into the sky and circled above the castle gardens. Then he flew back and settled on the windowsill beside Growl.

'That ought to do it,' he said.

The Bogle was feeling left out.

He knew that Semolina and Cat were cooking up something to help Midden's barbecue and he'd overheard Corbie discussing it with Growl outside the window. Why did no one ask him for help? He had his bag of magic dust where he always kept it, down the inside of his left Bogle boot. Midden had often explained that magic dust couldn't actually *do* magic, just make any magic more lively.

'That would be exactly right for a case like this,' the Bogle said to himself. He decided to follow Semolina and Cat out of the Magic Factory and into the castle gardens. Once there he waited until nobody was watching and then he sprinkled

 some magic dust between the bars of the grill rack that lay on top of the barbecue.

'That ought to do it,' the Bogle said happily.

The Bogle wasn't the only one who was feeling left out.

Over in the Swamp, Snap the Dragon had woken up and was feeling less cross. He sat at the entrance to his cave. It was lonely being a dragon. In the olden days there had been lots of dragons, but now there was no one around for him to play the good dragon games with, like 'Hide and Shriek' and 'Pin the Knight on his Horse'. Any time he tried to join in with other people they ran away screaming. Once he'd seen the children from the Multi-Story School out on a picnic. They seemed to be having a good time so Snap thought he'd go over and say hello. But when he'd thudded across the grass towards them Professor Pernickety had chased him off with a stick.

And as for that daft crow this afternoon, what was wrong with him? Snap had only been making fun when he'd mentioned toasted crow. As if a dragon would eat toasted crow! It would scarcely fill a hole in his tooth. But the batty bird had let out an earsplitting screech and flown away up the nearest tree.

Now Snap wished he was at the barbecue.

'I'll bet they're having a blast over there,' Snap sighed.

At that very moment in the castle gardens a burger blasted off the top of the barbecue grill. It rocketed into the sky and zapped Growl the Gargoyle right across his chin.

'Oi!' yelped Growl. 'What was that?'

The next instant a long stick of vegetables cata-pulted into the air. Slices of green, red, and yellow pepper smashed against the battlements.

Midden's mouth fell open. 'How did that happen?' she asked.

Before anyone could reply the barbecue began to glow with a fearsome fiery light.

'Perhaps we shouldn't have poured in all of that potion,' Semolina whispered to Cat.

Cat's whiskers trembled in reply. 'I feel a catastrophe coming on.'

Rat-tat-tat! A whole stream of prawns pinged against the windows of the Great Hall. Then a fat mushroom whizzed through the air and landed upside down on the head of Corbie the Crow.

'Suits you, Corbie!' Growl the Gargoyle gurgled with laughter.

'Cool, man,' agreed the Bogle.

Flames from the barbecue rose higher.

'Not so cool now,' said Jamie in a worried voice. 'Perhaps I shouldn't have used extra strength fire-lighters.'

'You used extra strength firelighters?' said Midden. 'I added a dozen Crackle Pops!'

'And we poured a Fizzing Fire potion over the coals,' admitted Cat and Semolina.

'And I used some magic words I got from Growl,' Corbie owned up.

Everyone looked at the Bogle.

In answer the Bogle held out his empty bag of magic dust.

Midden grabbed the nearby safety bucket of sand. 'I'm going to put the barbecue out,' she said. 'For when that lot heats up, there's going to be—'

The most enormous explosion rocked the castle.

* * * * * * * * * *

Snap could smell Midden's Midsummer
Barbecue food cooking.

And see smoke.

And flames too.

Snap frowned. There weren't supposed to be
flames at a barbecue. He knew that, because, when
he was younger, he and his friends held barbecues.
Every so often they'd get together and hang out
and belch hot flames at princess-shaped veggie
burgers. They'd chat and tell dragon jokes, and
laugh until smoke came out of their ears. Just the
way he could hear the people in the castle laugh-
ing just now.

Snap's head snapped up.

That wasn't laughter he was hearing.

It was screaming.

Something was very wrong at Starling Castle.

Inside the castle gardens Midden and her team were
fighting the fire with all their magic and non-magic
powers.

Semolina had turned herself into a hosepipe and was

drawing water from the castle well. Under Corbie's directions, Cat was spraying the water on the flames, but the flames were so big that they were getting closer and closer to the Great Hall.

Growl and Jamie and the Bogle were shovelling sand onto the barbecue, but even with the Bogle using his four hands the fire wouldn't go out.

Midden was waving her magic wand and shouting, 'Flippety Flop! Make it stop!' over and over.

Suddenly a huge shadow appeared above them.

It was Snap the Dragon.

At first Snap thought there was another dragon in the castle gardens.

Oh goody, Snap thought, someone to play with.

Then he saw what was happening. He saw the flames reaching out to burn the castle. He saw Midden and her team of magicians exhausted and about to be overcome. Then Snap saw something else.

He saw the water glinting in the pond just outside the castle wall.

Snap beat his wings and swooped low over the surface of the pond. He opened his great jaws and sucked in a gigantic breath. Holding the water inside his mouth, Snap flew back to the castle. He opened his mouth and emptied a ton of water on top of the fire.

Splosh!

He flew back and did the same again and again until there was no more water in the pond and no more fire in the castle gardens.

Everybody made a fuss of Snap.

'I always knew that dragons could start a fire,' said Midden. 'I didn't know that they could put them out as well.'

Snap was very pleased with himself. Once Jamie and the Magic Factory team had dried off, and Snap's throat had recovered, he even agreed to make some fire for a new barbecue.

As the dragon's flame-throwing wasn't up to full strength, Snap could only manage to make a tiny fire, but not a single person complained about that.

Theresa Breslin is a Carnegie Medal-winning author whose work has appeared on radio and television. She writes books for all age groups and they have been translated into a number of languages. She lives in the middle of Scotland, a short broomstick ride away from Stirling Castle. It was while visiting Stirling Castle that Theresa noticed something strange . . . Stirling Castle is very, very like Starling Castle where the Magic Factory workshops are. So keep a sharp lookout if you ever go there . . .

There's lots more 'Magic Factory' fun
to be had. Why don't you try . . .

## TRICK OR TREAT?

In another set of magical stories, Midden and her
friends must stop the terrible twins terrorising the
town; round up some runaway scissors; stop the school
from a spell disaster; and catch an invisible imp — all
before the big Hallowe'en party!

Let the Magic Factory cast its spell on you!

There's lots more 'Magic Factory' fun to be had. Why don't you try . . .

## COLD SPELL

Midden and her friends must warm up the prince of winter; untangle a magical mix-up; calm a cross dragon; and undo a dancing spell—and all before midnight!

**Let the Magic Factory cast its spell on you!**